Other Titles Available:

 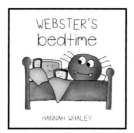 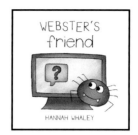

For Layla and Iris

Published by Born Digital Books.

www.borndigitalbooks.co.uk

First printing: September 2015.
Rudiment Font © Kevin Richey

ISBN-13: 978-0-9930012-5-3

Webster's Manners

Written and Illustrated
by Hannah Whaley

Webster was a good spider.
He always tried to be polite.

He thought he knew his manners,
but something wasn't right.

"I always seem to get told off
but I'm just playing with my toys."

It's 'Put that down!'

or 'Switch that off!'

'You're making too much noise!'

"Well," said Daddy Spider, "perhaps I can explain.
There is a time and place for everything -
then no one will complain."

It's important that you eat your meals.
You have to concentrate!

Anything noisy that flashes or beeps
will come after you clean your plate.

It's important to be ready on time, so if we're running late... anything noisy that flashes or beeps will always have to wait.

It's important that you talk to us,
so when we ask about your day...
anything noisy that flashes or beeps
should be put down right away.

It's important to look after things,
so if you are running when you play...

...anything noisy that flashes or beeps
should be safely tucked away.

It's important that you take a bath,
brush your teeth and wash your hair...

...anything noisy that flashes or beeps
will get too wet in there.

It's important that you get your sleep,
so when it's time to rest your head...

...anything noisy that flashes or beeps should be nowhere near your bed.

"Ok," said Webster. "I've got it now,
but so we both agree...

...if there's a time and place for everything, that doesn't just mean me?"

Like when you're cooking in the kitchen
and chatting on the phone to gran...

...anything noisy that flashes or beeps
should be nowhere near hot pans?

And when we're driving in the car (even if I made us late)... anything noisy that flashes or beeps will surely have to wait?

Or when I'm trying to ask you something and you say you're on a quest...anything noisy that flashes or beeps could surely take a rest?

When our bed time comes around
and it's up the stairs we go...

...anything noisy that flashes or beeps
should be turned down really low?

"I think that's everything," said Webster.
"I feel much better now."

"Um, yes..." said daddy, a bit confused.
"I'm glad I helped... "

"... somehow."

Made in the USA
Middletown, DE
29 November 2020